D1389186

Big Pancake to the Rescue

by Katie Dale and Steve Stone

FRANKLIN WATTS
LONDON•SYDNEY

This story is based on the traditional fairy tale,
The Big Pancake, but with a new twist.
You can read the original story in
Hopscotch Fairy Tales. Can you make
up your own twist for the story?

Franklin Watts
First published in Great Britain in 2015 by The Watts Publishing Group

Text © Katie Dale 2015
Illustrations © Steve Stone 2015

The rights of Katie Dale to be identified as the author
and Steve Stone as the illustrator of this Work have been asserted
in accordance with the Copyright, Designs and Patents Act, 1988.

ISBN 978 1 4451 4302 6 (hbk)
ISBN 978 1 4451 4303 3 (pbk)
ISBN 978 1 4451 4309 5 (library ebook)

Series Editor: Melanie Palmer
Series Advisor: Catherine Glavina
Series Designer: Peter Scoulding
Cover Designer: Cathryn Gilbert

Printed in China

Franklin Watts
An imprint of
Hachette Children's Group
Part of The Watts Publishing Group
Carmelite House
50 Victoria Embankment
London EC4Y 0DZ

An Hachette UK Company
www.hachette.co.uk

www.franklinwatts.co.uk

Once upon a Tuesday, a baker
decided to cook his biggest
and best pancake ever.
It was ENORMOUS!

3

He tossed it once, twice, then –
WHOOPS! – the pancake flew
straight out of the kitchen window!

"I'm free!" cried the pancake happily, rolling down the hill.

"Come back!" cried the baker, chasing after him.

"No way!" called the pancake, whirling down the hill. "I'm on a roll!"

"Come back!" cried the butcher, joining the chase.

"No way!" cried the pancake, whizzing down the hill. "Watch me fly!"

"Come back!" cried the candlestick maker running after them all.

"No way!" cried the pancake –
but suddenly he stopped rolling!

Then he started rolling backwards!
"Help!" cried the butcher as
the pancake rolled over him.

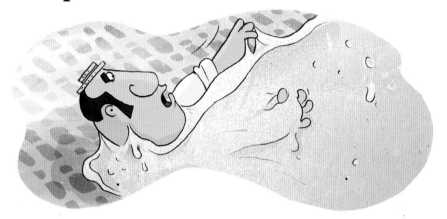

"Help!" cried the baker as
he got stuck too.

"Help!" cried the candlestick maker. "We're all stuck! And there's a GIANT!"

"Fee-fi-fo-fum!" cried the giant. "Dinner time! My favourite – a giant pancake – or should I say MANcake? YUMMY!"

"Help!" cried the men.

"Help!" cried the pancake.

But then the pancake had
an idea. He rolled away from the
giant. "You're not fast enough!"
squealed the butcher as the giant
gave chase.

"He'll catch us!" cried the baker.
"Look out!" shouted the candlestick
maker. "There's a RIVER!"
Sure enough, they rolled right into
the water – SPLASH!

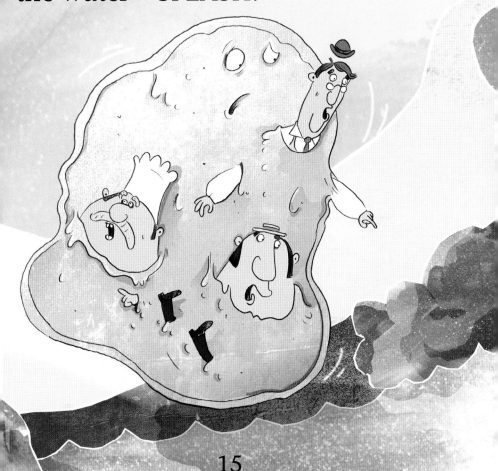

"We'll drown!" cried the butcher.
"I can't swim!" cried the baker.
"The giant's going to catch us!"
yelped the candlestick maker.

"Trust me," smiled the pancake.

The river was wide and the current was strong, but thanks to the pancake they all floated safely on the water.

The giant tried to chase them
as they floated away, but he
was too slow.

Finally they were swept to shore.

"We're safe!" cried the three men.

"Look, we're not stuck any more!"

The water had softened the pancake's batter, and they all pulled themselves free. "You've saved us, Pancake!" they cheered.

But the pancake was now soggy and full of holes and couldn't roll any more.

"Go home," he told them.
"I'm glad you're safe."
Sadly, he watched them go.

But soon the three of them
returned with a wheelbarrow
and frying pans!

25

Together, the townsfolk set to work repairing the pancake's holes, until finally he was even bigger than before.

27

The pancake jumped for joy and everyone cheered.

"Hip hip hooray for the biggest, brightest, very best pancake ever!"

29

Puzzle 1

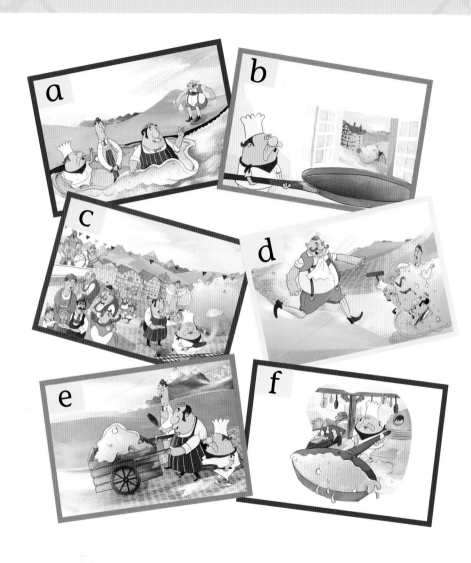

Put these pictures in the correct order.
Which event do you think is most important?
Now try writing the story in your own words!

Puzzle 2

Choose the correct speech bubbles for each character. Can you think of any others? Turn over to find the answers.

Answers

Puzzle 1

The correct order is: 1f, 2b, 3d, 4a, 5e, 6c

Puzzle 2

The baker: 1, 6

The pancake: 2, 5

The giant: 3, 4

*hardback

For more Hopscotch books go to:
www.franklinwatts.co.uk